Manuel Svenas -

Also from Jackanapes Press

Past the Glad and Sunlit Season: Poems for Halloween
by K. A. Opperman / Illustrated by Dan Sauer

The Withering: Poems of Supernatural Horror
by Ashley Dioses / Illustrated by Mutartis Boswell

The Voice of the Burning House
by John Shirley / Illustrated by Dan Sauer

The Ettinfell of Beacon Hill: Gothic Tales of Boston
by Adam Bolivar / Illustrated by Dan Sauer

October Ghosts and Autumn Dreams: More Poems for Halloween
by K. A. Opperman / Illustrated by Dan Sauer

The Miskatonic University Spiritualism Club
by Peter Rawlik / Illustrated by Dan Sauer

www.JackanapesPress.com
www.facebook.com/Jackanapes-Press

Praise for *Book of Shadows*

"No contemporary dark fantasist more ornately encapsulates or gleefully embodies in day to day life the Victorian Gothic essence than does Manuel Arenas. These funereal incantations are wrought of black, delicately faceted crystal, wherein one may see reflected the glossy black curls of Gothilocks, or the pale proud visage of vermilion-lipped Morbidezza. Femme fatales are the stars of this nocturnal pageant, but many a monster peer from these nightshade-tainted shadows as well. Like the sweet yet lethal berries of Atropa Belladona, these purple poems in prose and verse provide the perfect entertainment for an October night."

— K. A. Opperman
Author of *Past the Glad and Sunlit Season*
and *The Laughter of Ghouls*

"While there is no denying Manuel Arenas' devotion to the macabre, a definite strain of farcical absurdity runs through these pages, reminding us that horror and comedy are more closely related than some might care to admit. Owing as much to the influence of Edward Gorey, Young Frankenstein and the Addams Family as to more serious antecedents such as Poe and Grimms' Fairy Tales, this morbidly delightful collection of tales and poetry is sure to bring a rictus grin to all who read them."

— Adam Bolivar
Author of *The Ettinfell of Beacon Hill*
and *The Lay of Old Hex*

Praise for Manuel Arenas

"The poetry and fables of Manuel Arenas are like specially gifted party favours on All Hallows Eve. Unwrap them and you are regaled with black humour shot through with light…elegant beauty one breath from decay… quaint huggable little nightmares masquerading as words."

— Galad Elflandsson
Author of *The Black Wolf*

"A prolific writer of blacklight [sic] verse and satanic sonnets, he spends his nights sleeping in a coffin and dreaming of black leather Barbarellas and planets full of malfunctioning Edgar Allan Poe robots. His only known weakness is running water."

— Ashley Naftule
Phoenix freelance writer,
dramaturge, and performance
artist extraordinaire

Book of Shadows

GRIM TALES
AND
GOTHIC FANCIES

MANUEL ARENAS

ILLUSTRATED BY
DAN SAUER

JACKANAPES PRESS

Many of the tales herein have been revised for inclusion in this collection.
The following is a list of their initial appearances in print.

"Morbidezza" first appeared in *Spectral Realms* No. 10 (2019, Hippocampus Press)
"Vampire Vigil" first appeared in *Spectral Realms* No. 11 (2019, Hippocampus Press)
"Kiss of Life" first appeared in *Spectral Realms* No. 12 (2019, Hippocampus Press)
"The Baleful Beldam" first appeared in *Spectral Realms* No. 11 (2019, Hippocampus Press)
"Rosaire, Master of Wolves" first appeared in *A Walk in a Darker Wood* (2020, Oxygen Man Books)
"Greetings from Krampus" first appeared in *Spectral Realms* No. 14 (2021, Hippocampus Press)
"Satanic Sonata" first appeared in *Spectral Realms* No. 12 (2020, Hippocampus Press)
"Hell-flower" first appeared in *Spectral Realms* No. 13 (2020, Hippocampus Press)
"My Bantam Black Fay" first appeared in *Spectral Realms* No. 13 (2020, Hippocampus Press)
"Errant Jenny" first appeared in *Wyrd Folk and Wive's Tales* (2021, Frisson Comics)

First Paperback Edition
1 3 5 7 9 8 6 4 2
ISBN: 978-1-956702-02-6

Dedication

IN MEMORIAM
JOY BINGHAM STRIMPLE

Contents

Morbidezza & Other Denizens of the Dark Wood

THE SANGUINARY SAGA OF MORBIDEZZA VESPERTILIO, VAMPIRESS

OTHER DENIZENS OF THE DARK WOOD

The Misadventures of Gothilocks & Other Children of the Night

The Devil
& All His Works

Afterword

Illustrations

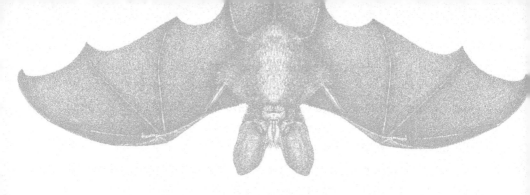

Foreword:
Dead Things Within

Around 2018, I became an avid reader of S. T. Joshi's journal of contemporary Weird poetry, *Spectral Realms*. A verse in issue number 9, titled "Thalía" and written by one Manuel Arenas, immediately caught my eye and aesthetic: a sumptuous vampiric banquet, featuring such lines as, "Between the curtain and the quick…"! Here was an immediacy of the grotesque, decadent sensibility paired to morbid speculation, the Gothic subsumed and transformed. I was hooked, and on the lookout for further work by this writer.

In subsequent issues Arenas began releasing his sequence of Morbidezza prose-poems, contained in this *Book of Shadows*, ensuring a fan in me. With each new installment he advanced a luxuriant entwining of beauty and the monstrous, telling the tale of a mighty vampiress kept in suspended animation, parched of blood, by a mortal lover (lest I reveal too much I'll leave it at that, hoping to whet the reader's thirst!). Arenas—known as Manny to his friends—and I struck up a friendly correspondence, trading writing, discussing our mutual love of the Weird, horrific, and Gothic. Eventually, I was honored to be asked to introduce this volume.

The poems, prose-poems, and stories contained herein read as arcane rites, incanted with a sorcerer's precision to terrifying and carnal affect. Reading them summons an imagined hint of opiate brazier-fume, coupled to the unmistakable stench of rifled charnel-houses; Arenas' creatures of the night are liberated, his demons gleeful and triumphant, works of black magic and diablerie encompassing the transcendent and profane in profound unison. Yet, there is also a sly sense of humor and irony, the ominous hint of French and German faerie-tales bound up in the skein, providing pervasive and dreamlike feelings of dread—especially when one fully surrenders to the lush lull of his language. Love and lust play their part, but there is an absence of sentiment, an unflinching validity of arresting image and incident. One could almost be examining the intricately carved lintel of a centuried tomb, rendered in written form; you can feel the rotten moss under your fingertips, hear the faint-but-restless stirrings of dead things within.

Manny's work is in the psychic vein of Poe and, perhaps most directly, Clark Ashton Smith—indeed, his "Rosaire, Master of Wolves" takes place in Smith's haunted French province of Averoigne. Other comparisons spring to mind, not least of which is Baudelaire, but the point lies beyond any stylistic or thematic juxtaposition. Arenas' writing is distinctly his own, distinctly wicked. His frequent twists on symbols of Catholicism (addressed here in "Nativity in Black: An Antichrist-mas Story") take the theme of sacred blasphemy to Boschean proportions; in another mode, the faerie-tale Goldilocks is reinterpreted as "Gothilocks," a ghoulish amusement sure to bristle the hair while eliciting a sardonic chuckle. Arenas' world is rich to abundance with bewitching danger: Black Goddesses wait enticingly in the shadows, hungry for blood, as Hecate's Hell-Flowers bloom by the roadside.

So, who is he, this mysterious Manuel Arenas, scribe of such dark and debauched verses as lie ahead? I could mention subjective traits (eloquent blogger, with an expansive taste in classic horror films and music; faithful correspondent and fellow Poet, owner of ebony locks and a wardrobe that put a certain Transylvanian count to shame; onetime front-man of The Dark Young, a Boston band who blend prog, goth, and avant-garde jazz; check 'em out on Bandcamp!), but the true summation is he is a devout practitioner in the grandest tradition of the Weird and macabre. And this is his Book of Shadows.

— Scott J. Couturier,
April 19, 2021

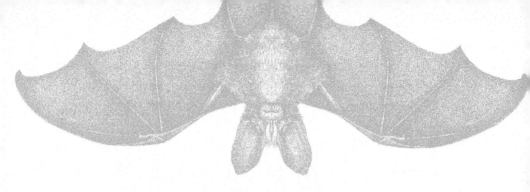

Introduction:
Book of Shadows

What is a Book of Shadows you ask? Well, ostensibly, it is a book kept by a High Priest or Priestess containing the tenets and rituals of a particular coven. If you're not a Wiccan or an occultist, you may have first heard the term mentioned on the WB TV show *Charmed* (1998). The origins of the concept are debated, but the term was popularized in the mid-20th century by Gerald Gardner, the Father of Wicca. When I first created my blog back in 2011 at the recommendation of my longtime friend Y-Mike Yesenosky, I racked my brain for a suitable title for a place where I could post my writings, reviews, poems, stories, &c., and then it hit me: *Manny's Book of Shadows*! It has since evolved over the years, as the site has become more of a medium to keep interested parties updated on my publication appearances. I have taken down much of my creative writing (upon the recommendation of fellow poet K. A. Opperman), as many editors apparently frown upon accepting work which has already appeared online, and so nowadays I tend to only publish reviews and the odd personal observation on there.

The collection you hold in your hands has gone through multiple incarnations and even saw a failed fundraiser in 2014, which fell far short of its $2,000 goal. At the time, I offered to return the funds I accrued, but all parties demurred saying I could apply it toward a future project. I promised that I would come through for them and, when I had something to offer, they would be the first to receive copies. Sadly, one of those donors, fellow Planet Poe trouper, actress Joy Bingham Strimple, passed away last Spring, precluding me from honoring my original promise. Hence, it is to the memory of her generous spirit that I dedicate this august collection.

Originally drafted as separate chapbooks, I have here combined three titles, *Morbidezza & Other Denizens of the Dark Wood*, *The Misadventures of Gothilocks & Other Children of the Night* and *The Devil & All His Works*, to create a book of spells and lore under the cognomen *Book of Shadows*.

Now that the prosaic genesis of this collection has been elucidated, it is time for me to give it a more proper introduction—something more compelling, more poetic—more *Gothic*.

I Bid You... Welcome

The proscribed volume that you hold in your tremulous hands comprises thirteen of my finest poems and prose tales—a devil's dozen, if you will—representing almost thirty years' worth of blood, sweat and tears... as well as a bit of henbane, datura and deadly nightshade. They are best read at twilight, that oracular time when all things are possible—especially such things as delineated in these sombre pages. Pour yourself a drink; an apéritif perhaps, or your favorite philtre, then settle down into a cozy chair and surrender to dark enchantment. I suggest only perusing a few poems at a time, as they are rich and nuanced for the discriminating reader. Savor each darksome verse or tale for a spell before moving on to the next one. However, should you find a narrative maleficent enough to induce a case of the vapors—or worse—know that you will then have learned the valuable lesson of many an apprentice mage: to not mess with tenebrous books, unless you are prepared to deal with the consequences. Good luck dear reader, good night... and don't let the vampires bite.

—Manuel Arenas

Morbidezza

& Other Denizens
of the
Dark Wood

The Sanguinary Saga of Morbidezza Vespertilio, Vampiress

Morbidezza

Immured within a tourmaline tower, the Vampiress Morbidezza Vespertilio waits. Weary and wan, she gazes through the silver bars at the crimson-colored glass of the lone tower window which keeps the deleterious sunlight at bay. Combing her silken sable tresses, she broods over her dispossession and personal losses as she tries to recall the aspect of spilt blood on a moonlit kill. She is allowed one book by her captor: a bible, which she largely ignores save for when she uses it as a *sors sanctorum* to divine auguries of her desiderated release. To while away the endless hours of her captivity, she plays her spinet and sings a melancholy monody for her lost love, Körbl Graf von Totenlaut, who was slain by Adalbert Glöde, a towheaded prosperous blacksmith's son and self-styled vampire hunter from Leipzig. He staked the venerable count as he lay, estivate and defenseless in his coffin, then decapitated him and stuffed his mouth with garlic. However, when it came time to dispatch his Venetian consort, beauty stayed the slayer's hand.

The inexpert young Adalbert was so taken by her luxuriant black hair, her exquisite pallor and scarlet mouth, he could not bring himself to destroy her. Instead, he bound her coffin in silver chains and kept it under a haystack in his father's smithy until he could build a small tower house with schorl transported from the Ore Mountain Range in Saxony, which he furnished with some of her belongings that he seized from the vampire's schloss. He erected the structure deep in a riparian forest, far away from prying eyes, and placed its entrance on the banks of the river so that if the lady found her way out of her confinement, she could not cross the threshold. The somber tower loomed forbiddingly beneath the crown canopy of the forest like a benighted beacon, its piceous walls barely capable of retaining the mortiferous miasma which seeped between its stones through the porous lime mortar blighting the adjacent demesne; felling all the flora save for deadly nightshade and repelling all the fauna save for those creatures which emerge after the vesper bells summon the faithful to eventide orisons; most notably a cortège of bats, which swarmed the structure, flying to the aid of their sovereign.

To curry favor with the lady, and at considerable cost to his depleted purse, he purchased an ornate girandole mirror from her native land, replete with candlesticks to light up her gloomy little chamber. When she espied it across the room, upon awakening from her diurnal repose, the lady overlaid it apace with a cramoisy mantle which suggested to him a cascade of blood. Abashed upon grasping his gaffe, he left for her a turtle-dove in a gilded cage as a peace offering, only to discover upon the morrow the headless, bloodless body of the little bird sprawled within the mangled cage. Conceding defeat, he swore off procuring anything else for the dark donna that she did not herself request.

Because his Lutheran sensibilities won't allow for the procuration of innocent blood for her profane sustenance, she has become etiolate, torpid, and to all appearances, exanimate. Yet underneath that lifeless façade her preternatural anatomy toils constantly to revivify her undead carcass as her demoniac mind cogitates on vendetta. Unsure of how to gauge her condition, Adalbert visits his captive daily in her solitary room and lights a spermaceti candle by her catafalque so that he may pore over her comely countenance, looking for signs of corruption whilst furtively pining for a return of her unnatural vigor. For hours he gapes at her black velvet voluptuousness and her necrophilic allure: her alabaster bosom, her pallid brow, and her mesmeric red mouth. The gelid touch of her marmoreal flesh causes a thrilling horripilation to surge through his piqued physique. Every day he stays longer and longer, lingering until his eyes start to grow bleary and flutter as the candle flame sputters into oblivion in a puddle of pellucid wax. And all the while Morbidezza's violet irids, ostensibly insensate, peer surreptitiously through the villous lashes of her creviced eyelids, awaiting the day when her besotted subduer tarries too long in his vigil, providing her an opportunity to exact her revenge under the sanguinary rays of the setting sun as it filters through the crimson panes of the tower window like a cataract of retributive blood.

Vampire Vigil

Slumped in a Luther chair, Adalbert Glöde, failing in his vigil, dozes and dreams of his inamorata, the Vampiress Morbidezza Vespertilio, who lies, quiescent, in her ebon coffin on an inky, satin-draped catafalque. Initially resolved to descry the stir of vitality in her marmoreal mien, he has instead nodded off, dreaming of her sepulchral pulchritude and wicked wiles. He longs to kiss her luring red lips and rekindle the vivifying ardor in her gelid breast, melting the preternatural derma-frost returning her milk-white flesh to its connatural suppleness that is consistent with her appellation, but dares not for fear of contamination from her unhallowed contagion. He craves her acknowledgment of the asseveration of his love, but her ire at his treachery will not allow for it. Believing her stuck in the pall between worlds of the living and the dead, he dreams that he seeks her accurst shade in the Underworld but has gone astray, meandering in the Mournful Fields. He calls her name but the only response amidst the keening din of the disconsolate shades of unrequited and slain lovers is the tinkling of his ladylove's spinet and the doleful ayre of a turtledove.

Wandering aimlessly through the bleak shadowland he spies the shade of his other victim, the Graf von Totenlaut, whom he smote when he spirited away his consort, that undead Delilah, lumbering amidst the pitiless fallow glebe-land bearing his severed head. He halts asudden and holds his head aloft from its raven locks, like a lantern, scanning the woebegone terrain till his embittered, silvery orbs rest upon Adalbert like fulgurating stars gazing down with fierce discernment. As the rent in his albescent breast gushes precipitously his heart's blood in a torrent, his gaunt, livid visage opens its fang-barbed lips to call out his slayer's name, "Adalbert!"

But the voice that emits from his ghastly maw is not the grave baritone of the once-stately count, rather the mellifluous, albeit minacious, intonations of his bewitching relict, the exquisite fallen angel, whose name is synonymous with death-warmed delicacy, yet whose heart is as black and implacable as the dreams of Death. He hears the voice again, but this time from all around him, as the articulation of a lowering deity lording over him from above. Straining his eyes in the adumbration, he tries to locate the source of the utterance. As oft happens in the absurd realm of dreams, the unlikely spectacle of the sanguinary cataract swells into a deluge, flooding the fruitless ground and overwhelming the spurned cavalier, covering him up to his neck briefly before he succumbs to the gory wave.

Waking with a start, Adalbert struggles to focus his bleary blue eyes to the grisly candlelit spectacle on his lap: a twined crimson mantle atop which is perched a mangled and masticated bird's head, a turtledove.

"Morbidezza!" he cries.

"Sono qui," returned the voice of Doom.

Kiss of Life

As Nótt rides her dusky steed across the Germanic empyrean, bringing night upon a riparian locale in the northern woodland, and wolf-driven Máni speckles the forest canopy in argent refulgence, an eldritch scene is brought to light upon the roof of a dark tower house. A supine beauty, her albescent flesh almost luminescent in the lunar lucency, lays straggled across the rooftop, her luxuriant black mane and velvet dress disappearing into the shadows leaving only the cast of her countenance to glimmer in the gloom like a fallen star. Her crepuscular eyes stare vacantly at her astral brethren, and they return her inert gaze in kind.

Her feint had worked; her foe had been lured into a false sense of security, overstaying his vigil, and she dispatched him with acute enmity, leaving nothing fit to return postmortem. Using her late captor's key, she frees herself only to find her egress impeded by the flowing river abutting the tower threshold. Not one to be deterred, she grasps the lintel over the doorway and pulls herself onto the face of the tower with what little strength remained in her ill-fed frame. Clawing her way to the rooftop surface she collapses, effete and bereft, resigning herself to follow the sylvan night-song into oblivion, and await the fateful dawn. Sensing her imminent demise, the woodsy denizens of darkness slither and slog from their bosky bowers, to keen for their moribund queen.

Howbeit, emerging from their perch under the eaves of the tower in a flurry of coriaceous wings, an umbra of fantastically large vampire bats scud across the face of the moon, momentarily eclipsing its silvery beams to alight upon the fading femme fatale. One by one they crawl, with wings outstretched, across her marmoreal mien to her pallid face and deliver to the ruddy mouth of their ailing sovereign a rivulet of vivifying blood, restoring the Vampiress to her preternatural fettle. Their errand betimes completed, the sanguinary retinue flaff and flutter off for a hemic nightcap ere repairing to their shuddersome cavern lair to roost and await their proximate summons.

Flushed with an evanescent quickening that gives her pallid cheeks a fleeting roseate hue which flares and falls like the death throes of a mayfly, Morbidezza exhales a dolent sigh, as a sanguinary tear exudes from her violet oculus. With the spryness of a cat she springs to her unshod feet with renewed élan and divests herself of her gore-imbrued velvet vestment afore running toward the edge of the tower rooftop from which she seemingly plummets into darkness... only to rise again and hover momentarily; her alabastrine thews, gleaming in high relief against the piceous cheek of the tourmaline tower, are held aloft by a pair of hellac-ious bat wings that flail the neighboring trees in the vortex of their wake and whip her sable tresses in writhing frenzy, causing them to coil and spring like black adders above her spectral brow.

Congregating around the blighted detritus of the tower demesne, the children of the night crow and kvell as their darksome mistress deigns to acknowledge their adulation; her erstwhile violet eyes, transmogrified to a candescent glare, beam like balefires in the mirk of the night-veiled forest. Then, with a thresh of her sooty wings she darts above the canopy of her blasted environs and soars into the moonlit firmament, like a fury loosed from Hell, with her sundered heart scabbing over with wrath and her morbid mind overbrimming with bloodshed.

Other Denizens of the Dark Wood

The Baleful Beldam

Anent a toadstool fairy ring, within a darkened wood,
A bothy, blighted, lies where bides a crone who bodes no good.
Her garden bears a noisome bed of noxious flowerets.
Her hearth has been the *mise-en-scène* of hellish *tête-à-têtes*.
Her cauldron roils with viands queer, you would not care to eat.
Contrariwise, she feeds her imp with blood from out her teat.
Her ruddled eyeballs barely see, but she can sniff you out;
Then snatch you up in her gnarled clutch to gut you like a trout.
Good many hapless mendicants have knocked upon her door,
Summarily ushered thither, then seen again no more.
Sometimes her shadow has been seen to dance in lunar light,
A-frolicking with woodland nymphs into the autumn night.
Upon the eve of All Saint's Day, she flies astride her broom,
And cackles as she casts a spell, with dolor fraught, and doom.

Rosaire, Master of Wolves

(For Galad)

I

There was once a young man who sometimes was not, and in these instances the ambit of his maleficia encroached way beyond the pale. His mother was a soothsayer-healer who lived on the outskirts of the village of Les Hiboux, in the French region of Averoigne, at the dawn of the Century of Lights, during which epoch Darkness still found a way to periodically rear its caliginous head. His father was a priest who called upon the cunning woman to bring her the Word of God. It is not known how well the Word was received, but idle prattle wending its way to the Abbey of Perigon was that the man of God was heard to call out His name several times during the protracted visit. To forestall any scandal, the Abbé Donadieu besought the diocesan bishop to send the priest to New France to get him out of the public eye, then quashed all residual strains of gossip at the source with threats of excommunication. Despite all the ado, the Lord of Hosts must have countenanced the hospitality the young woman showed His humble servant upon his mission, because she was soon blessed with a prima facie healthy child just in time for the proximate *Noël*. Howbeit the midwife, a village slattern who owed the young mother a favor, was a bit ill at ease with the breech birth and crossed herself after handing the rubicund newborn to his mother.

In honor of the devotional contrivance which lead to the conception of her beloved babe, the woman named her son Rosaire. He was a beautiful boy with a full head of lush auburn hair, ruddy cheeks, and amber-colored eyes. She loved her little cub and proudly sang his praises to whomever brought her custom. In time, he grew into a handsome and clever stripling to whom his doting mother inculcated the métier of her craft as well as what little she knew of faierie and the shadow world.

Motherly love notwithstanding, Rosaire grew to be of a saturnine humor which caused his mother some concern, so she suggested he divert himself with some playmates from the village, but the village hens would not allow their chicks to play with the by-blow of the priest and told them to steer clear of the witch's urchin with his furry brow and toothy smile. Taking their aspersions to heart, she pondered whether her boy was not truly marked for unpropitious fortune, and so one night, as he lay dormant before the hearth, she took it upon herself to look into his heart, with the aid of an obsidian palm ball, to divine what sort of man he was destined to be. Peering into its inky depths, she focused her thoughts on her slumbering cub but, to her dismay, found her efforts stymied by a tutelary spirit; a shadowy warden with fiery eyes, that guarded his latent nature like a Cerberus. As she pulled away from his redoubtable gaze, she envisaged an image of a funeral pyre, but dismissed it as a phantasm playing on a reflection from the hearth. Soon after, business began to drop as many of her former clientele became fearful of being seen at the "cursed hovel on the edge of the wood," so consequently, she was forced to take on some unsavory patronage which she would have formerly declined: skulking malefactors, calling under cover of night, requiring noxious philters and baneful charms.

During these calls Rosaire's mother would send him around the back of the hut to keep him hidden from esurient eyes. Ever and anon, upon conclusion of the nefarious dealings, the cunning woman would go to fetch her precious lad but would find him to have strayed, like as not to chase the prodigious toads which proliferated in the region, often not returning till the following morn. At first light she would find him curled up on his palliasse before the hearth, with his copper hair full of leaves and twigs, his pale face smudged with berries from the nearby brush, and his long nails encrusted with soil, like some wild child of the forest. On one raw November morning, however, she awoke to find her precious Rosaire with his erstwhile ruddy cheeks besmirched with gore and lamb's wool.

Fearing the windfall of woe following his discovery by some angry shepherd she grabbed her son by his rufous scalp and dragged him to the wash basin where she scrubbed him of the incarnadine muck from head to toe. During the ablution she discovered a supernumerary nipple on his torso, which hitherto had not been present on his wiry frame. She blanched and recoiled at its shivery touch, for she knew it to be the dread devil's mark, an ominous emblem of her son's befoulment by the unhallowed touch of the Archfiend. Again, she grasped him by his hair and demanded he tell her from whence he came by the noxious nevus. Rosaire then recounted the tale to his Maman of his misadventures in the phantom-haunted forest.

He told her of the swart Lord of the Forest, whose sooty chill hand he was bidden to kiss. He told her of daubing salves and donning skins, of rutting at revels and running with wolves. He told her how the Lord of the Forest saw how he was cunning and said that if he served him unwaveringly for seven years, he would grant him authority over his own pack, and they would rule the forest roads by night. His mother, dumbfounded, stared at her beloved cub, smacked him across the face, then held him to her breast as she bewailed the loss of his immortal soul.

Knowing that their time was limited before the aggrieved shepherd would be coming around with a posse comitatus to stir up trouble, Rosaire's mother adjured him to leave forthwith. She offered to pack him provisions, but he declined, saying that the Lord of the Forest promised that with his new coat he would always be warm and he would never want for victuals as long as he ran with the pack, under his auspices. Embracing him once more, Rosaire's Maman kissed her son goodbye and sent him on his way, after which she prepared for the direful upshot which was yet to come.

And come it did; first as the imprecations of an irate shepherd; then, as Rosaire's infamy grew, as the obloquy of the harried villagers. As Rosaire was under the protection of the Dark Lord, they could not requite their wrath on him, so they took the next best option.

II

Rosaire spent the ensuing perennial heptad terrorizing the woodland of Averoigne by night; riving bantlings, ravishing maidens, and ravaging graves in the service of the Dark Lord, during which time he was also instructed by his umbral lordship in the dark art of nigromancy. In those years he grew tall and brawny, and his chin lost its boyish smoothness as he became more than a youth, or a man for that matter. Upon the conclusion of his atramentous apprenticeship, he returned to his former abode beyond the woods to look in on his loving mother, only to find a razed ruin. Sifting and sniffing through the vestiges of his boyhood home, Rosaire found his mother's charred remains, which he carefully removed and inhumed with the pertinent obsequies. Determined to discover the transgressors, he used the forest lore his mother had taught him and lit upon an aggrieved hamadryad, whose sister had been lost in the ensuing conflagration, who provided the desired identifications. Grabbing what few keepsakes he could salvage from the debris, he returned to his sylvan lair where he gathered the appropriate ingredients for the shape-shifting ointment.

From his vile cache he pulled black henbane and deadly nightshade, mandrake root and the fat of an unbaptized babe, which he ground into a paste with his mortar and pestle. Then, stripping down to his natural state, he anointed himself with the resultant balm, donned the pilose coat of a black wolf and intoned the lycanthropic litany which consummated his transmogrification into a bloodthirsty beast, although when he turned, his coat was black but his muzzle, like his beard, was red, as if stained with the blood of his prey. He then summoned his lupine horde with a howl that resonated with equal measures of dolor and furor. Emerging from the dark recesses of their woody bowers, the bloodthirsty pack responded, snarling, their slavering jaws snapping with anticipation of the hunt. Whereupon their doyen, the *Meneur de loups*, led them on a sortie to the village of Les Hiboux visiting bloody death upon the households of all those who partook in the harrowing death of his beloved Maman. They swarmed their abodes; dashing down their doors, crashing through their latticed windows, rending their thatch roofs; no crevice was left unexplored, no creature was left entire. No man, woman, child, or beast was spared from the wrath of the werewolves and their rancorous, ruddy ringleader: Rosaire.

Unseen by the slaughterous brutes and their shrieking quarry, a dark figure surveyed the carnage from a vantage point in the nearby boscage; his rufescent eyes glowed in the darkness like smoldering embers which threatened to catch flame on the contiguous branches. The canny shade's frore desiccate heart vellicated with an aberrant warmth to see Rosaire weaned from mother's milk with the blood of his enemies and so, in a fleeting moment of mentorial gratification, he accepted his protégé's blood-soaked oblation and smiled.

The Misadventures of Gothilocks

& Other Children of the Night

Gothilocks

(For Jessica)

I

And so, they sat: The Count, the werewolf, and the monster, alternately staring at the dreary countenances of their compeers and the mean mess spread before them.

"What I would give for a nice young milkmaid to feed on," lisped the Count through his mustachioed overbite.

"Yeah," growled the werewolf, "and when you were done draining her, I could take her limbs to gnaw on, then salt the remains and hang them in the smokehouse for jerky!"

"Jerky would be nice," muttered the monster.

The werewolf, hirsute ears perked up to attention, rejoined, "I thought you were a vegetarian!"

"Yeah, well maybe I am getting tired of all this squirrel food, ever think of that?" retorted the monster. "I need to find something I can really sink my teeth into."

"Amen to that!" blurted the Count, raising a slender, albescent digit for emphasis, its pointed nail practically piercing a waxen stalactite from a guttering candle on a low-hung, folksy chandelier.

"Something with resistance, but that won't crack my brittle denture," the monster continued, as he absentmindedly ran his large, leaden hand along his broad, ashen jaw.

"Hey," his lupine messmate howled mincingly, "you're the one who said, 'I do not destroy the lamb and the kid to glut my appetite; acorns and berries afford me sufficient nourishment.'"

The monster, frustrated and allowedly embarrassed, clenched his teeth and, pounding his ponderous fists on the table, responded with an agitated "Arrgh!"

"Gentleman, please!" hissed the Count, "Why don't we go for a walk in the woods and work out some of this pent-up choler?" The other two mumbled their assent and off they went.

II

Gothilocks had lost her way in the enchanted forest looking for atropa belladonna to blanch her complexion, which just was not pale enough for her taste. Even though she was renowned for her dark tresses, which framed her lovely face in jetty ringlets, she secretly coveted the pallor of that bitch Faustine, who was so wan and willowy that she looked positively consumptive! "I'm going to achieve that ghostly hue someday," Gothilocks swore. "Even if it kills me!"

For a self-proclaimed "Child of the Night," the little darkling was starting to wax a shade worried now that she noticed the onset of dusk blanketing the treetops in heavy folds betwixt the grasping, bony branches. She had all but lost hope of finding her way back home in the dimming light when she came upon an ill-favored cottage in a clearing. Gothilocks felt weary and hungry, so she decided that, as this was the only shelter that she was bound to find so deep in the woods, she would go the vole and make her approach. Granted, it was a tad forbidding in appearance, but she would have to make do with what was at hand.

She caught a glimpse of her reflection in the twilit window (the view into which was obstructed by a crimson velvet curtain) and stopped to primp herself in anticipation of her audience with the denizens of this lowly hovel. She wanted to look her best so that they would automatically take her in on account of her exquisitely coiffed locks and fetching good looks. She stepped up to the weathered wooden door, grabbed the ornate metal knocker and rapped three times. Awaiting a response, she noted, to her disfavor, that the knocker was fashioned in the likeness of the lolling tongue of a leering devil, which caused her to cringe then throw a piqued glance at her lily-white hand.

No answer. Pulling a red silk kerchief from her satchel, she wiped her hand clean. Then, using it to grip the rude clapper, she tried again, only this time a little more forcefully, and to her surprise the door swung open! Drawing a deep breath, she restored the kerchief to its place, then pulled back the hood of her cloak, spruced up her corseted *décolletage*, and boldly sashayed across the threshold where she stopped for a moment, arms akimbo, to take in her surroundings and seek out a host to charm.

She hallooed into the antechamber, but there was no reply from within its shadowy stillness. Advancing with caution into the dining room, she noticed an oblong table covered in a gray linen cloth, with three places set for supper, lit by a *lüsterweibchen* chandelier that barely illuminated the gloomy scene with its expiring candle nubs. The fixture featured a painted wooden figurine of a pallid, raven-haired woman resting on a candlebeam fashioned from a pair of deer antlers. On her crown she bore a diadem with a silvery orb flanked by crescents. In her left hand she held aloft a flambeau and, in her right, a coat of arms bearing a skull and crossbones. "How tacky!" Gothilocks snarked, eyeing it with disdain.

At one end of the table was a shallow metal bowl with a viscous red fluid in it. She looked to the side of the bowl but saw no utensils. Screwing up her doll-like features to inspect the ruddy contents of the bowl, she mused, "What is this, borscht? Nope, there's no sour cream, it must be gazpacho! Either way, I don't do cold soup, and this stuff looks like it's starting to congeal."

Spying something beneath the clotted surface she grasped the bowl by the edges and gingerly sloshed its contents to reveal the alarming high-relief image of a face devoid of any features save for a gaping mouth. Spooked, she resiled, dropping the bowl, which caused some of the fluid to spill onto the tablecloth, leaving an incarnadine splotch. Taking a deep calming breath, she moved on to the next place where sat a wooden dish with a large bone that bore several sizeable and unsightly tooth marks on it, indicating that it had been chewed voraciously by something with a measurable bite.

"What, they let the family dog eat with them at the dinner table? Ew! Wait, is that a femur?"

Disgusted, she pushed away the bone and went to the last place at the table, where she found a bowl full of what she assumed to be trail mix. Figuring this was as good as it was going to get without any hosts in sight, she ate it all up, and washed it down with a swig of bottled water from her satchel.

Feeling sleepy, she plodded up the alternating steps of the narrow staircase leading to the dormitory quarters in the loft. There she saw a coffin, which she climbed into precipitously, because she always wondered what it would feel like to be in one. However, it proved far too unnerving for her liking, so she clambered out in a trice and, stumbling, landed her derriere on a straw-filled mattress. The palliasse served well enough to break her fall but was repellant with animal sweat and shed hair, so she quit it posthaste.

Lastly, she came across what she took for an antique bedstead that had a bolster pillow at one end, but no bedclothes. Presumably the mattress had been the one she had just vacated; no doubt removed due to its doggish taint. Although it was a bit unyielding in its design, the frame reminded her of some minimalist accommodations she had seen once in a magazine.

"This is no worse than my box spring at home," she thought and, pulling her cloak close around her fatigued frame, she removed her high leather boots, stretched out her stockinged legs and was soon asleep.

III

Now the night was waning, and our boys were flagging from trudging around the forest and venting spleen, so they agreed to head back to eat their meagre supper and retire before the looming cockcrow. Upon arrival, they were flummoxed to find the front door to their creepy cottage ajar. Filing one behind the other, they entered with caution, the palpebrous Count leading the way, arm braced forward and ruddled eyes peering out from between his grizzled brow and his heavy black cape. The werewolf followed at his heels, beady black eyes narrowed, snout a-snarl, claws out for an attack, and the monster trailed behind, his yellowed eyes wide as doubloons, nervously scanning about the chamber, like an oversized and misshapen boy, frightened out of his patch-worked gourd.

In the main room, where their meal had been set, they found a sight which caused the trio some concern and, for the monster at least, a great deal of dismay.

"Someone has spilt my plasma potage!" cried the Count, incredulously.

"Someone has been hovering around my marrowbone, I can smell it!" growled the werewolf.

"Someone has eaten all of my muesli," sobbed the monster, "Now I won't have anything to eat for supper tonight!"

"Don't worry, *mon frere*, all is not lost," the werewolf said to the monster as he patted his elbow reassuringly with a hairy, black-clawed hand, "for I smell an intruder in our midst!"

The werewolf then led his unearthly friends up the staircase into the loft where they found a disturbing scene.

Recoiling as if from a crucifix (aghast at the thought of a plebeian desecrating his immaculate crib), the Count gasped, "Someone has been in my coffin!"

"Someone has been snooping around my pallet!" gnarred the werewolf irately.

"Yeah, well someone has been sleeping on my slab … and they're still there!" bawled the monster. "Where am I going to sleep *now*?"

The eldritch trio stood around the monster's bier and marveled at the beauty of their uninvited guest.

"Boy, she sure is pretty," the monster mumbled, as he rubbed the tears from his eyes and wiped his sutured nose on his frayed, dingy coat sleeve.

"Yeah, her hair is so black and shiny," said the werewolf in a hoarse whisper, "I just love the way the curls frame her perfect little face, I mean *look at that skin*, white as alabaster!"

"I've seen whiter," the Count interjected, "but yes, she is a fine specimen."

The werewolf grinned a toothy smile, and with a hint of a snarl in his voice, slyly uttered, "Are you thinking what I'm thinking?"

The Count, leering, licked his livid lips in response, as the monster turned to regard his comely usurper and affirm, "Jerky."

Belladonna

I

O nce upon a time, not so very long ago, in a town devoid of strip malls, there lived a young lady named Faustine. Not having been born with much good sense, but somewhat blest with good looks, she focused all of her energy on enhancing and maintaining her physical appearance.

Faustine was popular with the local youths, whose obsequious flattery and flirtation were the only attention she ever got in her lonely adolescent life. Her sole rival in this respect was a haughty young coquette named Gothilocks, who was renowned throughout the region for her jetty locks and fetching good looks. One evening, in the closing days of September, as Faustine arose with the setting sun, she stood at the railing of her balcony looking onto the forest and poised within the twilight moment, made an oath to the murky woodland and its inhabitants. She swore that she would give anything to find a secret that would cause her beauty to surpass all others—especially that horrid wench, Gothilocks.

Then, just as the sun finally gave way to his mistress, a tenebrous figure stepped out of the woods and encroached upon the grounds leading to Faustine's balcony. Faustine was shocked by the stranger's boldness, and yet entranced by her grace. She was impressed with her confident stride and almost funereal solemnity of mien. When the mysterious personage came in close enough, she pulled back the tulle of her wide brimmed hat and revealed herself to the young lady, who was amazed by her beauty; startled, in fact, to the point of almost being aglifft. She was a perfect vision of sepulchral pulchritude, clad in a form-fitting dress of dark purple velvet. Her skin was unnaturally fair, her lips were thin, but nicely formed, and seemed to be painted a dark reddish color, turning to black. Her arresting gaze, as she turned it toward Faustine in the half-light of dusk, showed irids of an almost black color that, in truth, were rather of a deep purplish hue. She had high cheekbones, which protruded slightly, insinuating a death's head; nevertheless, she was breathtaking.

Faustine stood there, spellbound, and gaped at the figure with what must have really been a silly expression on her face, because the moment was soon shattered by the snickering of the stranger. This rattled her from her reverie, and put her on her guard.

"Who are you," demanded Faustine, "that dares to trespass onto my land and laugh in my face?"

"My name is Atropa Belladonna and I beg your pardon, but I was in the vicinity and could not help but hear your plea, and felt impelled to come to your assistance."

"That's a very strange name," she said, "and I'm not supposed to talk to strangers."

"O darling lamb," she intoned in a voice sweet as aspartame, "do not be sore with me. I heard you bleating, as a shepherd hearkens to an errant charge and must come to its aid and show it the way. Dear sweeting, allow me to help you in your endeavor, and I promise you shall become the most beauteous babe in all the land."

"More beautiful than Gothilocks?"

"Who, that curly-cued cow?"

"I like the way you think, and your offer is tempting, to be sure. May I have a day to sleep on it?"

"You may have a day to think on it, wherein you may sleep upon what or whomsoever you please, but I must have an answer by tomorrow evening just after sunset. Then, if you consent, we may begin to transform you into the envy of every girl, and the desire of every swain in town."

"On second thought, I'd rather not wait. I want to start being beautiful now!"

"Do you not wish to consult someone before making your decision? Your parents, or perhaps a confidant?"

"Why, so she'll learn my secret? No, thank you—and besides, I never talk to my parents. The less they know the better; they've even said as much themselves. No, I am quite sure in my decision. I wish to start now."

"We have not yet discussed the cost of my services..."

"I don't care, I've got money to spare. I'll do it no matter what the price!"

"Very well, then," said the stranger, with a smirk. "We begin tomorrow at the previously appointed hour. I shall arrive just after sunset, and you shall follow me to my home where I shall wait on you."

Then, bidding Faustine a good evening, the stranger slowly slank away, vanishing into the woods. Almost immediately thereafter, our ingenue started to have doubts about her decision, and wondered if she hadn't acted too hastily. She even reconsidered telling her parents, but then thought better of it.

"Oh well," she reasoned, "She seemed nice enough; besides, anyone that pretty can't be so bad."

II

The following evening, at the pre-appointed hour, Faustine met up with Ms. Belladonna, who led her to a secluded area of the woods where the ground was damp and sunlight scarce. There, in the middle of nowhere, was a curiously quaint little cottage, which was surrounded by a singular looking plant with puce-colored flowers and dark purple berries, which brought to mind the purpure of the lady's dress.

As they entered the house, the girl noticed an inanimate rabbit by said plant with purple stains on its paws and mouth. Turning to her hostess, she asked what was wrong with the creature.

"The little minx has no doubt eaten its fill of my uniquely potent berries, overtaxing its digestion, and therefore must sleep it off. Naughty cotton-tail!" she said in a huff, as she flounced past the threshold of the cottage. Eyeing the still creature as she followed, Faustine just could not detect any sign of breathing from the little lagomorph.

When inside, she was surprised to see that there was no kitchen. Nor was there any indication of any kind of comestibles ever having contaminated the place. There was no bed either, only a large armoire, a vanity table, surmounted by a rather large and ornate mirror, and two chairs all made from ebony wood. She was seated in one of the chairs, which was accented by purple velvet cushions.

"Omigawd," thought Faustine, "Mircalla and the others would positively die for a chance to sit in a chair like this!"

So it was, that then and there, Faustine was turned into a Gothic princess. She was shown how to henna her hair that copper color she'd been trying to master all summer long. She was shown how to blanch her skin, as well as tastefully apply the more somber-hued cosmetics. She was also given free rein to try on any of the dresses in Ms. Belladonna's wardrobe; and when she got up the nerve, she even dared to try some of the leather accessories the lady had fitted especially for her little dress-up doll. She didn't have any PVC wear though, the lady did not approve of it: "I never don it, and neither should you; it is not natural!" she opined. Apart from this small disappointment, Faustine was looking great—and feeling great too!

As she looked at her reflection in the mirror, she was speechless. She had always been a pretty girl, but now she was a goddess! The gentlemen callers would be tripping over themselves to ask her out, as well as some of the more venturesome girls, and—best of all—she would make Gothilocks look like a carnival-grounds-haunted-house reject!

"For the finishing touch," cooed the lady, "a few drops of my special ointment in your eyes to enhance their natural brilliance, and you can be on your way." Leading Faustine back to her chair, and leaning her head back, she squeezed the bulb of a small dropper into the young girl's eyes, then kissed her on the forehead as she closed her lids to ensure the capture of every drop.

As she stepped back over the threshold to leave, Faustine was startled to see what appeared to be a swarthy baldpated man, dressed in black trousers and a gauze shirt of pale green, which was not unlike the color of the flowers of the plant growing alongside the dwelling. His pronounced collar furthered this likeness, causing his head to inevitably suggest the fruit of the plant. She surmised that he wore dark-colored clogs but could not quite tell in the gloom. He struck an imposing figure, standing by the hedge, glowering, with a pair of clippers in his left hand. Gasping, Faustine stepped back and put up her hands to protect her pretty little face.

Then she heard the derisive laugh of Atropa Belladonna, mocking her fear, as she approached from inside the cottage.

"Funny little moppet, do not be afraid, that is only my familiar, Banewort, come to help me tend my herbs. He's a charming old devil, once you get to know him, and he is so dedicated to those plants! You know, he can only be persuaded to leave them for one night a year, just before May Day."

"A religious observance, you understand," added the fellow in a peculiar accent, as he advanced toward the flustered Faustine. "It just wouldn't do for me to miss it." His complexion, upon closer inspection, was of a darksome puce tinge, which she dismissed as a trick of the gloaming. His features were odd and hard to place. He was anthropomorphic yet did not seem to show any identifiable attributes of any ethnicity. However, there was something feral in his countenance, which gave an unsettling aspect to his smile, and made him all the more frightening when he scowled.

Faustine stared for a moment as Banewort's smile grew into a leer, goading her to blurt out, "I must go home now." And so, she did.

III

For the next several evenings, Faustine found her way to the lady's home without an escort. On the way, she came across many a young buck who offered to walk the demoiselle through the perilous woods. Ms. Belladonna, however, had expressly forbidden her to let anyone know where she was going, or whom she was going to see. Faustine didn't mind though, she liked having secrets to lord over the other girls with. She also relished all of the attention she was getting and took joy in seeing Gothilocks fuming at her physical transformation and newfound popularity.

In fact, she was even approached by Gothilocks, who feigned friendliness in an attempt to extract her beauty secret from her. But all she could get out of Faustine was a smug smile and her reply, "Why, Belladonna of course!" This somewhat cryptic answer left her rival so perplexed and annoyed that she could strangle the glossy-eyed bitch. Where could she obtain this belladonna, and what exactly was it? More importantly, what was its cost? Come Hell or high water Gothilocks swore, she was going to find out, even if it was the last thing she did. But that's another story.

Things were really going quite well for our little darkling. She was looking the best she'd ever looked. This gave her more confidence, which brought her more attention, and in turn detracted from Gothilocks's popularity. This made her very happy indeed.

And yet, even though she was happy, after a spell, she started not to feel as well physically. In fact, she started to feel quite ill. She began to get headaches, and her mouth was always dry. She ran a fever, her throat burned, and she had trouble swallowing.

Even so, she continued to visit Ms. Belladonna as a daily routine, to get her primping and dosage of drops. She would drag herself to the little cottage in the deep of the woods, feverish and heart pounding as if it would pop, practically collapsing on the threshold to the woman's oversized closet of a home.

Then the lady would take her protégé by the hand, and with her support and steady step, would walk her over to the vanity and tell her in soothing tones how beautifully wan she looked as she combed her long coppery-colored tresses.

"Why my dear baby bat, you look so lovely and pale. You are the physical dichotomy of life and death. You are the Gothic ideal of vivacious beauty and mortal corruption. You are my spiritual child!"

(Faustine cringed a little at this last statement because, "I mean, come on, what real Goths would ever call themselves one?")

"Yes, but Ms. Belladonna..." she began.

"Please, Atropa."

"Atropa... I have not been feeling well lately."

"Are you not happy? Are you not satisfied with the results of our sessions together?"

"Well, yes, I am... but..."

"But what my dear? Come, do not worry your little head about such things; worries wreak wrinkles. You have probably just caught a chill whilst carousing about town with your many suitors. I trust you have some now—more so than before, I mean?

"Well, yes, but..."

"But nothing! I grow impatient with your carping! Do you want to be beautiful or not?"

"Yes."

"Do you want to be desirable or not?"

"Yes."

"And do you want to outshine Gothilocks or not?"

"Yes!"

"Then quit puling like a whelp and sit still so that I may put these drops in your eyes!"

Faustine, envisioning the face of her rival, contorted with jealousy and bewilderment, acquiesced.

IV

When she left the lady's abode that night, Faustine could barely walk. She stumbled in the doorway and slumped down to the floor. She felt hot and flushed, so she pushed back her cowl, and pulled on the front of her corset to let in some of the cool night air. She felt delirious and faded in and out of consciousness. After a moment in oblivion, she opened her eyes to find Banewort's frightening face just inches away from her own. As usual, he was smiling, which always turned up his features in a rather unsettling way. His breath seemed to engulf her in a fog of sickeningly sweet pungency.

"What is the matter my little sweeting? Do you not feel well?"

"My head pounds like a taiko drummer and I feel sick in my stomach."

"Ah, perhaps you are hungry. Please, let me get you something to eat. I have some fresh berries here that I have picked and cleaned just for you. I had intended to give them to you before but wanted to make sure that Ms. Belladonna would permit it, as they are her berries after all."

"Berries? Are... are they safe?" said the ailing girl, with much diffidence.

"Are they safe! Really my dear, what you must think of me! Would I ever hurt you? Have I ever hurt you? Watch me; I'll eat one—nay, a handful. Watch!" Having said this, Banewort savagely shoved a bunch of the purple-cum-black berries into his maw and chuckled oafishly as the juice dribbled out of the side of his mouth in inky streaks, which could only be seen by their reflection of the moonlight on his dark features.

Faustine took a few of the berries, and with some degree of trepidation, put them in her mouth. As she began to chew, she was surprised by their sweetness, and, as she swallowed, began to think to herself how silly she... had been... to doubt...

V

When she came to, on a leafy bed at the edge of the forest, Faustine thought she saw the faces of her parents, who had come to save her, and take her back home to cherish her, their estranged but beloved daughter. Cruel clarity, however, soon revealed the gloating faces of Banewort and Atropa Belladonna. Moving in close, the lady took Faustine gently by the hand and with an earnest and imploring look said, "Tell me, sweeting: were you truly happy with the things I gave you? I hope so, because, as you see, the cost of my services is very dear indeed." Then, with a smile and a kiss, she rose and sauntered away with her fiendish friend in tow. And at those parting words, Faustine, abandoning all hope, relinquished consciousness and fell into a deep sleep, from which she never woke, as the first rays of the morning sun insinuated themselves through the treetops and onto her pretty pallid face.

Errant Jenny

There once was a young reprobate from London named Owen Lowell who, after a bad scrape with the authorities in his hometown, had decided to lay low in the countryside and rusticate till the dust settled. No, I won't divulge the exact location, to deter anyone from replicating his misadventure. He kept his nose clean for a while, but old habits die hard and one night he got antsy and decided to tie one on at the local public house. He wasn't there for long when, deep in his cups, he got handsy with a barmaid and was booted from the premises. Traipsing drunkenly out of the pub and into the surrounding boscage, he wandered deep into the woods just as the sky was reddening and the sun relinquished its grasp on the sky to the darkness of night. Stopping to relieve himself on a tree he thought he heard the faint murmur of voices wafting within the rustling leaves on the chill autumn evening breeze. Turning to see from whence it came, he spied a flurry of lights which anon coalesced into a single beam headed directly towards him. He feared on the spot that he'd been caught by the local constabulary: nicked, bang to rights, for public indecency. However, he soon discerned the figure of a young woman, holding aloft a lantern and humming a dissonant lilt to herself as she jauntily made her way towards him in unshod feet. He thought for a moment that he should hide anyway, as he didn't need any more trouble that night but, no matter which way he crept, she always seemed to turn in that direction. Eventually, he gave up and stood still, waiting for her to come upon him.

"Well, hello my lovely!" he said upon her arrival, "Good thing you came when you did; I wandered into the verge for a slash and seem to have lost myself in all this timbre. Would you be a dear and direct me to the main road?" asked he, with a bow and a wink.

She spoke not a word in response, but smiled and motioned for him to follow her, which he at first did gladly, until he realized that they were just going deeper into the forest. He attempted to point this out to the young woman, but she did not appear to pay him any mind. He watched her, as she glided through the forest, between the trees and brush without much thought or effort. It was difficult for him to keep up with her, but he followed apace as best he could, for he now had ulterior motives.

She had a sylphic figure that Owen covertly took stock of, draped in a light-green muslin dress, which clung complimentarily to her lithesome body. Her long reddish-brown hair, parted in the middle, fell past her shoulders in a cascade that glinted a coppery resplendence in the shimmering lantern light. Her general bearing made him wonder if she was feeble-minded. She perambulated in a world of her own, her viridescent eyes staring wistfully into somewhere other than their respective surroundings. She had a wide mouth with full pink lips, which smiled vacantly, and fair skin, with a sparse sprinkle of freckles that he thought looked like fallen leaves afloat in very still water. In her hand was a lantern fashioned from twigs, held together with spiders webs, and lit by what appeared to be fireflies, that shown dimly in the obtenebration. He began to worry that they were lost, or at least he was. His guide was taking him down unbeaten paths, twisting through odd byroads, yet he got the distinct impression that they were just travelling in circles. He wondered if she was mad, some bedlam escapee, and whether he'd ever find his way back to his temporary lodgings in the village.

As if surmising his train of thought, she turned around at that precise moment and gave him what she must have intended to be a reassuring smile, but rather had the adverse effect on Owen's well-oiled nerves; and would she never stop warbling that damned song? At this point he was getting frustrated. If he wasn't going to pull this bird, maybe he needed to push a little to inveigle her into seeing his way. If not, all he wanted to do was get through this darksome wood and sleep off his drink. He felt enervated, not a little fuddled, and he could swear he still heard muted voices yammering somewhere nearby. What were they saying? He swore he could almost discern a name being muttered repeatedly amidst the ululation.

Before he realized it, he found that she had led him straight to the rim of a murky pond, partially obscured by a layer of bright green duckweed, which wasn't very broad, but was seemingly deep. His guide had stopped her tune (mercifully), and carelessly dropped her lamp onto the forest floor, where it broke apart, allowing its glimmering captives to burst into the air like sparks from a smithy's anvil, accompanied by a muddle of murmured voices. Curiously, rather than dispersing into the forest, they drifted toward the pond and hovered just above the surface of the water. She then turned around to face him with outstretched arms staring at him with those empty eyes that reflected the dark fathomless semblance of the subfuscous pond and, smiling, pulled him to her pallid bosom. She kissed his cheek, then slowly moved towards his mouth. He felt a prickle of anticipation as her lips brushed against his own. His heart pounded as she held the back of his head with her right hand and wrapped the left one around his waist. For a moment, he was lost in pleasurable feelings and thoughts as he eagerly reciprocated in kind. However, when she pulled away, he saw, to his horror, that her lips were blue and her face puffy and discolored. Her hair was tangled and riddled with pond scum. She smiled again, a dead, soulless grin. Owen screamed, but she placed two water-logged fingers with loosened fingernails (one on the verge of coming off) to his lips, playfully shushing him like a leman would a recalcitrant swain. He tried to disengage himself from her grasp but found her grip to be firm and vise-like. She forced his head upon her shoulder in a vitiated attempt at consolation and resumed singing her cursèd song as she receded into the deep of the pond, dragging him along with her.

Terrified, he swore a blue streak, calling her all manner of colorful epithets, demanding she let him go, but she just persisted in trilling her irksome air as she pulled him into the algid deep of the pond. His panic waning to acceptance, Owen then saw the glowing lights more closely and realized that they were not fireflies at all, but corpse fires, lambent lost souls, and in his final terror, as his throat filled with noisome water and his brain fought for oxygen, Owen's terminal epiphany was that the disconsolate voices he had been hearing were emitting from the tiny spectral flares, wailing mindlessly in misery the name of their mistress. And as he shed his mortal coil, his immortal soul was compelled to join the chorus of disembodied animas who, like him, had the ill fortune to hearken to the discordant strain of Jenny, the fell maid of the drowning pool.

The Devil

&
All His Works

In Central European folklore, Krampus represents the shadow side of the Yule Time celebrations. An anthropomorphic goat/demon, he goes about punishing naughty children with his switch, the worst of whom he binds in chains, sticks in his basket, and drags to Hell. He is celebrated December 5-6, and, in the Germanic countries, it has become customary to send Krampuskarten (Krampus Cards) depicting lurid scenes of Krampus either chastising children or frolicking with buxom Fräuleins. The common salutation on these cards is Gruß vom Krampus (Greetings from Krampus).

Greetings from Krampus

At this joyful time of year, full of festive reveling,
There is one whom you should fear if you are prone to deviling.
On the heels of blithe St. Nick, comes a fellow dark and wild,
Horned and beastly, like Old Nick, who seeks a naughty child.
Cloven hoof and lolling tongue, with a basket on his back
Filled with wicked Alpine young, wailing at his switch's crack.
Lapping at their bleeding welts, their cries foment his thirst,
Heedless of their rueful guilt, doomed in demon's clasp they're curst.
After which they're borne to Hell, shackled in a clanking chain,
On a sled of ne'er-do-wells, never to be seen again!

Satanic Sonata

It is late in the year, on a pitchy night over the potter's field in a small New England cemetery. The vault of heaven appears moonless, starless, and smothering in its blackness, which hangs like a funereal mantle over the unconsecrated grounds where lie, uneasily, the disconsolate shades of the wicked and unwanted. Beyond the unmarked plots of the indigent there is a rumbling tremor in the grounds as a fissure forms in the unblest soil of the quarter reserved for criminals, suicides, and decedents of questionable virtue or creeds. Gradually increasing in size, the rent erupts into a sizeable crevasse, belching forth reeking clods of burning sulfur and blue flames.

Like smoke from snuffed-out candles, anguished souls rise in phantasmal wisps; summoned from their cold carcasses, they wail in unison a single woeful plaint before being snatched into the abyss. Emerging from the pit are two Hell-born sons, their seared hides bearing a ruddy hue. The first, a long-shanked sinewy devil with a mannish head, grins a toothy smile; his yellow eyes staring at the empty spaces between the licks of flame as they lap at the perimeter of the pit. Perching on the shoulders of a headstone of a burking resurrectionist whose infernal punishment is to remain in his perpetually putrefying cadaver, the devil scrapes and scratches a discordant air on a fiddle made of coffin wood and strung with the innards of a sinner. Like a leering grotesque, he squats, stock-still, as his bow arm flails frenziedly at his sepulchral instrument.

Across the chasm, facing the fiddler, is a stubby devilkin with bovine features and ossicone-like protuberances on his brow. In his chubby hands he holds a large, curled horn hewn from the skull of a massive and unfamiliar creature. His languid eyelids half closed, his expression almost serene, he purses his lips, protrudes his bulbous paunch, and blows a dirgeful tone which rattles the remains of the abutting boneyard tenants. Mingling with the cloven-hoofed din is the pitter-patter of raindrops from a sudden cloudburst, sizzling as they dissipate on the parched rictus of the minikin hell-mouth providing a continuo accompaniment for the cacophonic recital.

But the downpour proves to be no match for the doomful gripe of unquenchable fire and shadow as it swirls from out of the brimstone pit to grasp at the ethereal quarry within its forbidding clutches, and the diabolical duo's tuneful profanity whirls across the tenebrous welkin, even unto the main kirkyard, to lacerate the peaceful slumbers of the goodly dead.

Ḥell-Ḟlower

At Hecate's prompt, Hell-Flower blooms:
Ray florets open, awash in streams,
Of moonshine splayed athwart crumbling tombs,
Dappling headstones in argent beams.

Bathing in full moon luminescence,
Wafting in the fetor of Hell-mouth breath,
Perfumed airs of graveyard putrescence,
The potpourri of decaying death.

Drawing sustenance from coffined ground.
Fecund, yet foul, beyond potter's field.
Stretching its roots in unhallowed mound,
Cornucopia of unclean yield.

Puce petals frame a floral death's head,
Smiling with teeth absorbed from the soil.
Gnawing morsels purloined from the dead,
Wriggling amidst defiled charnel spoil.

My Bantam Black Fay

I have a little manikin that sleeps inside a cask,
I feed him blood from my left hand; he does then what I ask.
He follows me where're I go, perdu to all but me.
Occulted from the Christian eye thro' impish sorcery.
Conflagrant eyes mine mesmerize with their perfervid glance.
His silver tongue glints as he speaks to cinch me in a trance.
He whispers secrets in my ear, to make one's hair turn white,
then whisks me off on leathern wings to join a black mass rite.
He'll raze your home and salt your fields; he'll even taint your well.
He'll change your children out for sidhe, then drag your soul to Hell.
He's my infernal pedagogue, a boon from my Dark Lord,
and when I'm burning at the stake, he's sworn misericorde.
His name is unpronounceable for human tongues to say,
so, I just call him by the name of My Bantam Black Fay.

Nativity in Black
An Antichrist-mas Story

As the Doomsday Clock tolls the fateful hour, mystagogues turn their backs on the supplications and suffering of the laity. Christians decry prophecy, then cry fatefully, "These are the End Times!" as they await the Rapture. World leaders spew xenophobia, homophobia, and misogyny from their bully pulpits, as the sheeple cower in fear of losing their significance in a changing world. Allayed by fatuous beguilements, they willfully turn a blind eye as avaricious whistle-stoppers divest them of their entitlements and civil liberties and allow their children to be sacrificed to special interest groups, like Canaanites offering their young to the fires of Tophet in tribute to Moloch.

In this hour of darkness, a coven of Spanish witches was celebrating an *akelarre*, a black mass, in a remote cave in the vicinity of Zugarramurdi, in Navarra, Spain, when they were interrupted by the unexpected arrival of an emissary from Hell. Naked and dreadful she rose from the blaze of their bonfire, her long red hair cascading down the entirety of her pearly flesh to rejoin the flames, her green eyes fierce and dazzling. The witches were sore afraid and trembled at her approach, but she opened her palms at her sides and in tones of surety set their minds at ease:

"Fear not my little darklings, I am Lilith, true first woman and Queen of all Hell. I bring you good tidings that will be a boon to all children of darkness. Tonight, in the ruins of Chorazin an oppressor was born unto you; he is the Antichrist, your Overlord. This will be a sign to you: You will find a baby swathed in shadow, reposing in a minikin ebon coffin."

In response to her announcement a host of cherubic heads on bat wings sprung from the fire whence arose their mistress. Their lambent eyes glimmered like tiny candle flames in the gloomy cave as their red mouths chaunted in antiphonal response, "Hail to Satan in the lowest chasm, and on earth woe to those who incur his wrath."

At the conclusion of her annunciation Lilith raised her arms from her sides, flames appearing on either palm as she declaimed, "Let these lights become a beacon for all who wish to undertake the Black Pilgrimage and witness the beginning of the end." Clapping her hands together the flames coalesced to form a fireball which she released into the heavens beyond the cave. Simultaneous with the egress of the beacon was the withdrawal of fair Lilith and her dreadful chorus, followed by a return of the lackluster normalcy of the sublunary realm.

At the departure of the infernal host the coven rallied to choose three of their thirteen adherents to follow the *ignis fatuus*: the high priestess, a witch, and a warlock, who were disrobed and anointed with a supranatural balm. The priestess was given a trident, and the other two besoms, which all three mounted and rode like hobbyhorses into the frigorific ether where they soared across countless leagues of bible black welkin, disrupted solely by the gleam of Lilith's beacon, which burned always just beyond their reach.

The night air chilled their sky-clad bodies to the bone as they converged upon their bourn, and the temperature dropped precipitously when they struck a veritable wall of fuliginous feculence that nearly knocked them off their mounts with the strength of its mephitis, to tumble down miles of inky firmament to be dashed on (or drowned in) whatever lay below them. Recovering from the carom, they were approached by a monstrous fly that broke through the murky barrier, its compound eyes glimmering in a cluster of garnet fulgence as it cautioned the trio in a voice that shook the jostled witches with the force of a thousand bass racket horns.

"If you favored three were to intrude upon this Unholy Occurrence without the aegis of my infernal guard, your lives would be forfeit and your souls gnawed forevermore by the hounds of hell." As if on cue, the atmosphere cleared to reveal a grim legion of wingèd grotesques, gnashing their teeth and thrashing the air minaciously with formidable talons. "But come, fey mortals," the beastie added, "follow me to the cradle of your undoing, you are expected."

The trio braced themselves and followed the demonian insect as it plunged, in fleet descent, onto the site of the fabled ruined synagogue of Jacob Ory, shrouded in a cocoon of atramentous shadow. Presently, the elusive beacon reappeared in the caliginous heavens above the ruin before plummeting toward them, like a comet. Frozen in mingled fear and grim anticipation they followed its decent until, at the last moment, it slowed to alight on the flambeau between the horns of a terrible, anthropomorphic coal-black He-Goat who was the first to appear in the formerly occulted tableau which was suddenly illuminated before the dais in blasphemous splendor. His rutilant eyes smoldered with an ardor of infernal embers.

Acknowledging the pilgrims, the Light-Bearer deigned to motion for their approach. The witches, complying, were awestruck at the scene before them. To the left, lurking just beyond the fulgor of the He-Goat's beacon, stood a coterie of ashen-faced men in tailored suits. Each one in his livid hands bore a bauta mask adorned with the semblance of a human face, each vizard representing one of the sundry races of humankind. Their red eyes smoldered in the shadows as their forked tongues slithered betwixt their acuminate choppers.

To the right was a menagerie of benighted beasts: a stupendous toad squatting and squinting, its cat-like eyes surveying the coven with a scrutiny that betrayed an aberrant intelligence; a three-headed serpent, reared upright, with its heads thrown back, exposing its belly in obeisance; and an enormous black hound with a single flaming red eye in the center of its forehead which stood menacingly as acting sentinel to the infernal infant in the funest cradle before them. Next to them, a band of sooty devils created a discordant din: one blew a steerhorn from his buttocks, another played a tabor and a third a viol, all fashioned from human bones, gut, and skin.

Opposite them, genuflecting to the unholy family, were the bedeviled shades of the three magi: Ostanes, Zoroaster, and Hystaspes, granted leave from their underworld abodes to present the Satanic neonate with individual gifts of goety, astrology, and prophecy. The child's mother, a callow and corrupted apostate, was fair of face, lithe in figure, and arrayed in black. Crowned with a star-ruby in a silver diadem, she accepted their gifts with unseemly gusto, submitting each to her consort for his consecration before placing them on the dais.

The hell-bound Hadûi, with hesitant steps, approached the little black funerary box lined in black silk where an august newborn, swaddled in a protective wreathe of tenebrosity, gurgled and wriggled before opening his penetrating black eyes to regard his menials, who quailed at his uncanny gaze and fell on their knees to grovel.

Seeing this, the unhallowed cabal burst into a collective chortle of repugnant cachinnation, and the cat-eyed toad croaked with a loathsome intonation that caused the servile pilgrims' flesh to crawl. "See how they kowtow to their new Lordling? Soon all mankind shall show him deference thusly; for he shall be a mighty man with all governments of the civilized world in his pocket, and he shall hold sway over many nations. He shall be a treacherous counselor and an indomitable foe. He shall be the branch from which sprouts myriad pestilent fruits. For he is the Spoiler, the Son of Perdition, the Beast of the Pits—he is the Antichrist! All hail the Antichrist!"

At the cacodemon's prompt the monstrous menagerie erupted into a dreadful and cacophonous clamor before falling into the boisterous and blasphemous revelry of the inaugural Antichrist-mas saturnalia. The abominable infant cooed and squealed with something approximating mirth as the black nimbus enfolding his tiny body spilt over from the rim of his ebon cradle in tenebrous tendrils, radiating outward to the four corners of the earth like a funereal pall enshrouding the hearts and minds of humanity in a morass of anguish and despair.

Afterword

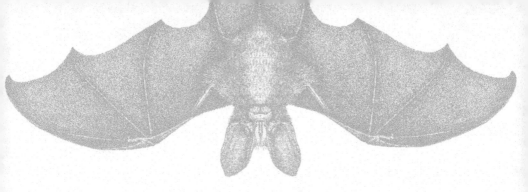

Tales from a Brother, Grim

As far back as I can recall, I have been fascinated with two things, Fairy Tales and Gothic Horror. I grew up watching the Universal and Hammer Horror films, and eventually sought out their literary origins. When I was a tween, my mother introduced me to the works of Edgar Allan Poe, which I read voraciously and which, after a while, inspired me to try my hand at writing my own poems and tales in his dark romantic style. Alongside my interest in the Gothic was my love of fairy tales, particularly those of the Brothers Grimm and Charles Perrault. I love their forest imagery and their admixture of folk tradition, whimsy, and primal horror. When I started to write my own stories, I wore my influences on my sleeve; but I am far from the first to marry these elements.

As I have said elsewhere, another great inspiration for my own *Antimärchen* (anti-fairy tales: i.e., gloomy stories with unhappy endings) are the tales of English author Angela Carter, whose book of re-imagined fairy tales, *The Bloody Chamber* (1979), has been exemplar for me in my own quest to create a flawless hybrid of the Gothic and the Fae. Her exquisitely written retellings of famous *contes de fées* by Charles Perrault, Jeanne-Marie Leprince de Beaumont, & al. with their unique blend of fairy tale, feminism, eroticism, ribaldry and Gothic Horror were the impetus behind my first forays into the genre, like "Gothilocks" and "Belladonna," respectively. I have been trying to write like her for 25 years now and have yet to come close. Even so, I persevere, and when

I decided to put together a sampler of my recent work, I opted to pull together all my prose tales and poems that have that Gothic fairy tale feel to them.

First off, we have "The Sanguinary Saga of Morbidezza Vespertilio, Vampiress." I had come across the word *morbidezza* in 2012. The word generally refers to a delicacy, smoothness, and softness of complexion and sometimes carries a negative connotation referring to sickliness and unwholesomeness. I immediately tried to incorporate it into a poem—although, even then, I was using it as a proper noun.

Fast-forward to 2018 when I decided to try my hand at writing an ornate vignette or prose poem in the style of Clark Ashton Smith. I wanted to write something very delicate and archaic sounding. I wanted it to be belletristic, metaphorically nuanced, and historically accurate. I had a vision of a fairytale princess locked in a tower by an infatuated suitor, like the Grimm Brothers' "Maid Maleen;" only this princess is a vampire. Recently, I have wondered whether, in a contemplative moment during the writing process, I might have subconsciously conjured the spirit of Erzsébet Báthory, the "Bloody Countess," who was walled up in her room as punishment for her allegedly bloodthirsty crimes.

For reference on folkloric vampirism, I consulted *The Vampire: His Kith and Kin* (1928) and *The Vampire in Europe* (1929), both by Montague Summers. For random historical detail I just trawled the Internet. In retrospect, I must have had specific tropes in mind when writing because I see multiple references to some of my favorite romances that should have been obvious to me, yet I was unaware of them at the time. Reading it now, however, I see thinly veiled references to J. Sheridan Lefanu's vampiric novella *Carmilla*, and Edgar Allan Poe's "Morella" as well as "The Masque of the Red Death." The same goes for "Vampire Vigil," the sequel to Morbidezza, which picks up from where the latter left off, only this time following the de facto villain of the tale, Adalbert Glöde, who is a not-so-charming variation of the besotted prince from the Grimm Brothers' world-renowned fairy tale, *Schneewittchen* ("Snow White" to you and me) who is so smitten with the moribund beauty that he had her glass coffin carried around by servants everywhere he went so he could continually gaze upon her comely pallid countenance. There is also a little of Nikolai Gogol's "Viy" (1835) in the mix, which is another tale of a vampire vigil of sorts.

Subsequently, I found that I hadn't quite finished with the Venetian Vampiress and wrote a third vignette, "Kiss of Life," to effectively tie up all loose ends in the original tale and give it a sense of closure.

Similarly, I turned to Montague Summers' treatise on lycanthropy, *The Werewolf* (1933) for Rosaire, in particular the story of the infamous 17th century teenage werewolf, Jean Grenier. The setting, however, is the fictional French region of Averoigne, created by the 20th century fantasist Clark Ashton Smith. Again, I strove for historical accuracy with the obvious exception being the fantastic elements. The third act, with the sortie on the village, was inspired in part by an analogous scene in the dark fantasy novel *The Black Wolf* (1979), by Galad Elflandsson, to whom I dedicate this tale.

As a little segue in between I have placed the poem, "The Baleful Beldam," about a witch who lives in an enchanted forest. On reflection, it seems all the pieces in this collection take place in Old World European forests. "Morbidezza," in a romanticized version of the *Leipziger Auwald* in Germany, "The Baleful Beldam" in an enchanted forest in Britain, and Rosaire in Clark Ashton Smith's fictionalized version of the Auvergne in France. I see these as Gothic Fairy Tales, written with an eye toward tradition, yet with the knowing wink of a modern practitioner of the genre. These are not for children, obviously, but rather for the discriminating adult who enjoys a little dark romance and fantasy with their fiction. I hope I have been successful in combining these two not-so-dissimilar elements into a satisfying entertainment with which one may wile away the hours with some mulled cider on a chill autumn night.

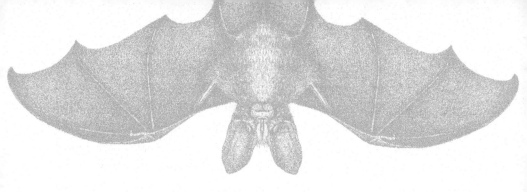

Mannymärchen

I first began writing in earnest around 2000 AD, when I penned a story for my creative writing class at Broward Community College (now simply Broward College) in Ft. Lauderdale, Florida. My professor, poet Michael Minassian, who I am still in touch with these 20-odd years later, once explained to the class the concepts of the protagonist and the antagonist, then mentioned how some scholars have an ongoing debate over who the protagonist is in the fairy tale "Goldilocks and the Three Bears": is it a story of a little girl who gets lost in the woods then takes refuge in a home which turns out to be inhabited by bears? Or is it a story about a family of bears that has their home invaded by a squatter while they're away on a stroll? He then had us write our own tale using the Goldilocks scenario as the basis. Being blessed (cursed?) with a Gothic imagination, I see the world through a purple-tinged lorgnette and thus the bears transmogrified into three thinly-veiled classic monsters and the golden-haired interloper was reborn into the night as a raven-haired Goth girl.

The story went over well when read aloud in class, as it was dialog-heavy and wickedly farcical. Inspired by my nominal success, I wrote two more tales in that universe: "Belladonna" (a prequel of sorts) and "Felo-de-se." In 2006 I collaborated with Phoenician Jesus "Jesse" Gutierrez, amateur cartoonist and founder of Bandido Studios, to create a comic book adaptation. The comic was a departure from his usual fare, which generally leans towards Mexploitation, featuring pistol-toting *cholos*, buxom *hynas*, lowriders, luchadores and Mexican movie monsters. Jesse used to have "spokesmodels," which were essentially lady friends whom he had don Bandido Studios t-shirts and pose as characters from his comics for signings at the local comic bookstores. He suggested I get someone for Gothilocks, so I asked my friend Jessica Garcia if she would mind dressing up as our sassy ingénue for the odd event and a few photo shoots. She consented, so I took her shopping for the costume, and even bought her a custom cape for the role, which she took to with gusto. Last we spoke about it, she said she still had everything packed in a box for safekeeping.

In the second run of the comic, we did a photo cover featuring Jessica, which had a teaser on the back for a version of "Belladonna" that was planned but never produced, featuring my dear friend Shawna Morrison. Jesse did an impromptu photo shoot for it with her when we were hanging out at her father (our buddy Rand Lyon)'s house. It was done on the fly with a black dress, a lacey shawl, a studded choker, and some make-up she had lying around. Nevertheless, I think it came out rather well! I had planned to do a series of chapbooks in the style of the Penny Bloods of yore, which I suggested we call *"Pesodillas: Pesadillas por un peso."* I wrote a series of cliffhanger stories for it, continuing the misadventures of Gothilocks and her fey pals, but our respective visions clashed, and the project floundered till we eventually went our own ways.

Over the years I have considered turning the initial tale into a picture book, like the puppet fairy tale books of Froebel-Kan, or maybe a puppet play, or even a stop motion film! I recently pulled out the tale to review prior to submitting it to a classic monsters anthology (sadly, it didn't make the cut), and quickly realized that it required both an update and some fleshing out. What you see here in this collection is a much darker tale than the original, replete with occult symbolism, sinister allusions, and dark mordant humor.

I have attempted to clean up the other two tales but made a point of keeping the flavor of the original drafts, so I beg your indulgence for their innate awkwardness and naiveté. Belladonna is a traditional style fairy tale about a neglected young woman who learns some life lessons the hard way: firstly, to never trust strangers; secondly, how beautiful people are not always good and, moreover, that the singular pursuit of beauty at any cost may result in dire consequences. Looking back, I see that Atropa Belladonna has some of the physical characteristics I later imbued in Morbidezza. If memory serves, the inspiration for her initial entrance in the story was the woman with the veiled picture-hat in the Steve Ball cover art for the 1997 vintage concert box set, *Epitaph*, by King Crimson.

In the story, I had a rabbit die from eating the belladonna plant; then I found out that, although not recommended, rabbits can indeed eat belladonna which they somehow detoxify internally post-consumption. Hence, I had to adjust it so that Atropa's brand would be a little more potent than normal to justify the rabbit's demise.

Like the Lord of the Forest in "Rosaire, Master of Wolves," the character Banewort is based on the folkloric Black Man of the witches. In the original version of "Belladonna," he was blackavised with ferine features. However, with the recent reckoning of old racist tropes this figure has become very controversial, so I thought that, in this instance at least, there was no real reason for him to be there unlike in "Rosaire," which is based on historical lycanthropy cases that specifically mention him, as in the case of Pierre Bougot and Michel Verdung in *The Book of Werewolves* by Sabine Baring-Gould. Consequently, I rewrote Banewort as baldpated and purple-hued, his head resembling the belladonna fruit, thus cohering his connection to the plant. To be honest, mayhap naively so, I never saw the relation betwixt the folkloric figure and the racist tropes until I read online where some people had retroactively called out H.P. Lovecraft's usage of the Black Man as an avatar of Nyarlathotep in "The Dreams in the Witch House."

You see, when I was a little boy, I saw some terrifying shadow things lurking in the corners of my bedchamber under the cover of night and so, when I later came across the trope in vintage supernatural tales, such as Washington Irving's "The Devil and Tom Walker," I never questioned that he was anything but darkness incarnate. To boot, in recent years, I have been told on a couple of occasions by different soothsayers that I have a tutelary spirit of sorts which manifests as a dark guardian that limits access to anyone trying to get into my spiritual inner workings. It has appeared to one reader as a black dragon, and to the other as a tall shadowy personage, the latter being a partial inspiration for the Lord of the Forest in "Rosaire."

I recall reading once, on some bygone blogpost, that the fruit of the belladonna plant is known in some lore as the Devil's Cherries, and there is a tradition which holds that the Devil himself tends on them nightly save for once a year: Walpurgis Night.

"Errant Jenny" feels a bit out of place to me, alongside the other *Manny-märchen*, because when I wrote "Gothilocks" and "Belladonna" I had in mind that their milieu was in some alternate version of New York, which I always thought of as Gotham (Washington Irving's Gotham, not the Gotham City of DC Comics) whereas Errant Jenny was crafted in loving imitation of an English folktale or traditional ghost story taking place in a romanticized version of rural England. It is essentially a folk-horror tale featuring an unseelie fairy based on two different creatures named Jenny from English lore: Jenny Greenteeth, and another, the sobriquet of which escapes me, that leads lost souls with her lantern off cliffs, like a will-o'-wisp or hobby lantern. I had intended to save "Errant Jenny" for a proposed future collection, but at the request of my colleague, Scott J. Couturier, I have instead included it here, where it replaces "Felo-de-se," a story set within the Gothilocks universe, that deals with the subject of suicide. The latter is the most ambitious of these tales, yet it is also the most uneven as it bounces wildly from fairy tale, to ghost story, to allegory, to farce, &c. I am attached to it, because it reflects the perturbation and conflicted emotion that I was feeling at the time I wrote it. Even so, I sent it to Scott for a proofread and his pragmatic assessment of it helped me come to terms with the fact that despite the rewrite, it does not hold up as an artistic statement and would put a blemish on this collection of what I deem to be some of my finer moments. If this book is well received, I may include "Felo-de-se" in a book of miscellanea somewhere down the line or, better yet, I may pilfer more bits to create newer and improved pieces. "Errant Jenny" is one such excerpt that I revised and refined. I am embarrassed to say that there is a version of it floating around in the ether that contains some imprudent attempts to incorporate English slang terms which, in retrospect, are cringeworthy and come off a bit like the American character in Bram Stoker's otherwise diverting slice of gallows humor, "The Squaw." After multiple rejections, I toned down this aspect of the story and Jenny was finally accepted for publication by Frisson Comics for the folk horror issue of their *Knock Knock* series, entitled *Wyrd Folk and Wive's* (sic) *Tales*.

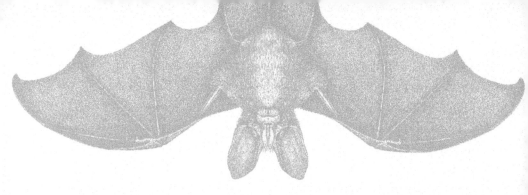

Diablerie

When I was a boy, I had a pocket-sized catechism book which I never really read; however, I do recall being a little obsessed with an illustration therein depicting the torments of Hell. It was a three- or four-color illustration of a leering Pan wielding a trident in a pit of flames that strategically lapped at the writhing fleshy figures of sinners doomed for eternity. If memory serves, there was a caption that read something to the effect of "Good children do not need to fear going to Hell." Well, I was terrified of going to Hell, did that then mean that I was not a good child and therefore fated to fry no matter what?

Although my family regularly went to mass on Sundays, ours was a secular household. As I grew older, I began to see the hypocrisy of your average churchgoer and by the time I left home at the age of eighteen, I had left the church behind entirely. Even so, I am still haunted by Catholic Guilt, and I have always been keenly aware of the mysticism and morality of my former faith lurking somewhere in between the lines of my dark fantasy tales, evidenced by my fixation with the personification of evil. I would not go so far as to call my stories morality plays, but the concept of choice and consequence does seem to be a prevalent theme, and people who do bad things are punished, more often than not. That said, the clergy (when they appear) are ofttimes ineffectual or even sinister. I mercifully never experienced any of the abuse that many have spoken up about in recent years and which has tarnished the good name of the Catholic clergy, but I do vividly recall one brother who brought me to tears by brutishly poking at my chest with his pudgy finger whilst browbeating me over some minor transgression. I have been chary of them ever since.

I have always been fascinated by the Dantean descriptions of Hell and the myriad demons that inhabit it, which I believe is borne out by the stories and poems contained in this little collection. We begin with a ditty I wrote for a Christmas-themed absurdist theater performance for my friends at the Space 55 playhouse in Downtown Phoenix. They asked me to write a song about the yuletide demon, Krampus, but I took so long to compose it they went ahead with something else entirely. At least I have this poem now, which has become something of a holiday favorite. In 2018, Arizona artist Dick Kelly and I put together a limited edition illustrated chapbook of the poem. The preamble was written at the behest of *Spectral Realms* editor S. T. Joshi, as an explanation for those who might be unfamiliar with this Central European phenomenon. When I wrote "My Bantam Black Fay," I had in mind *The Disrespectful Summons* by Edward Gorey, as well as a character from an unfinished story I had been working on that is a variation on the fairy tale "The Master and His Pupil."

"Hell-flower" is a companion piece to an earlier poem I wrote in the early '90s called "Flower of Evil." I jokingly refer to the pair as my horror-ticulture poems. Hell-Flower was inspired by the prose poem "Flower Devil" by Clark Ashton Smith. When "Hell-flower" appeared in *Spectral Realms* No. 13, I realized that the penultimate line ended with the wrong word, spoiling the rhyme. After consulting with Mr. Joshi about it, I checked my original draft that I had submitted, and it seems that in my haste to get out my revision I had mistyped the line myself! Lesson learned: always double-check documents before submitting them for publication. Of course, the correct word has been restored in this edition. "Satanic Sonata" was inspired by a fantasy I dreamt up while listening to "universal" (sic) by avant-garde violinist Evynd Kang. An earlier draft also included a prelude describing a singular scene I once witnessed in the 90s at the Old Burying Ground (est. 1635) between Christ Church (1760) and the First Parish Unitarian Church (1833), in Cambridge, Massachusetts, where a bevy of unruly pre-school kids were running amok amidst the olden gravestones as their guardians scrambled to collect them. I decided to dispense with it though, when I was cleaning up the prose to submit it for publication, as it had no bearing on the main narrative.

Last, but certainly not least, is the hero piece of this collection, "Nativity in Black," inspired by the song "N. I. B." by Black Sabbath. I was driving in my car listening to the song when I began to think about the story behind the title: it was initially a throw-away title referencing drummer Bill Ward's beard, which apparently looked like a pen nib. Bassist/lyricist Geezer Butler added the periods after each letter as an arch jest, but of course when the song hit the States, there was much speculation over what the title might mean, and someone somewhere began the rumor that it stood for "Nativity in Black." That is when the idea hit me, but it wasn't until sometime later when watching my DVD copy of *The Omen* (1976) that the idea really began to take shape. In the end I wrote a prose fantasy about the birth of the Antichrist, which initially mirrors the bible story of the nativity, then devolves into a veritable pageant of diablerie.

The story bears the subtitle: "An Antichrist-mas Story." I put a hyphen in there to allay any confusion for the zealots, who will most likely denounce me anyway for propagating anti-Christmas sentiment. Confessedly, it is a glorified flight of fancy about the birth of a baby boy... who just happens to be the Antichrist.

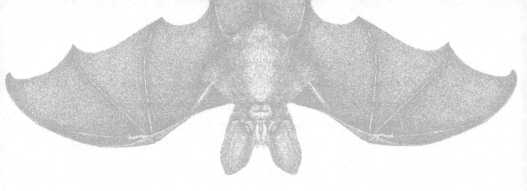

Gramercy

I would like to thank a few people who helped make this book possible. For starters, I would like to thank the poetess, Miss Ashley Dioses, who first encouraged me to submit my poetry to the journal *Spectral Realms*, and who also helped me refine "The Baleful Beldam" until it was in suitable shape to submit to editor S. T. Joshi, who also made suggestions which I took to heart. I thank Mr. Joshi as well for his subsequent support and sage editorial advice on several of my published pieces.

I would like to thank fellow Weird scribes Chelsea Arrington, Frank Coffman, and Scott J. Couturier for their support and advice on several of the poems and stories in this collection. Special thanks are due to Adam Bolivar for a last-minute proofread, as well as his informed suggestions for improving the meter on several of the poems. And extra thanks to Mr. Couturier for putting up with my maudlin missives, constant requests for beta readings, proofreading and for writing the introduction to this collection.

I would like to thank Mr. Derrick Hussey, founder of Hippocampus Press, for graciously allowing me an eleventh-hour re-write of the ending of "Kiss of Life" for its publication in *Spectral Realms* No. 12, which helped to make it the ersatz cover story for that issue, by default. I would like to thank Mr. Ashley Naftule for the wonderfully droll author bio that he wrote for a performance I took part in many moons ago and which I have resurrected for the encomium section of this book. I thank author Galad Elflandsson for his friendship, support, and the lovely blurb, which he originally wrote for a collection of my early poetry entitled *Black Hymeneal*—which I have yet to release—but the contents of which I have pilfered for this collection.

I would like to thank my friend, author Clint Werner, whom I first met as a customer when I worked at Half Price Books, and who has been supportive ever since I let it slip that I had ambitions as a writer. I would also like to thank my bosom friend, self-published author Zachary Strupp for his unwavering support, invaluable advice, and technical assistance in assembling the manuscript for this collection. Shout out as well to my friend Zac Besore for his help in proofreading earlier manuscripts.

I would like to thank my good friends Michele Bledsoe, Denisse Montoya, and Savannah Nangle respectively, for their friendship and hard work on earlier incarnations of this collection. And last, but not least, I would like to thank Dan Sauer and Jackanapes Press for taking on my little book and helping me realize a dream close to three decades in the making.

About the Contributors

MANUEL ARENAS is a writer of verse and prose in the Gothic Horror tradition. His work has appeared in *Spectral Realms* and *Penumbra*, respectively, as well as various genre anthologies; including *The Phantasmagorical Promenade*, *The Averoigne Legacy*, and *Knock Knock: Wyrd Folks and Wive's Tales*. He currently resides in Phoenix, Arizona, where he pens his dark ditties sheltered behind heavy curtains, as he shuns the oppressive orb which glares down on him from the cloudless, dust-filled sky.

SCOTT J. COUTURIER is a poet & prose writer of the Weird, liminal, & darkly fantastic. His work has appeared in numerous venues, including *The Audient Void*, S. T. Joshi's *Spectral Realms*, *Eye To The Telescope*, *The Dark Corner Zine*, *Space and Time Magazine*, and *Weirdbook*. Currently, he works as a copy & content editor for Mission Point Press, living an obscure reverie in the wilds of northern Michigan with his partner/ live-in editor & two cats. His short story collection, *The Box*, is forthcoming from Silent Motorist Media, and his collection of autumnal and folk horror-themed poetry, *I Awaken In October*, is slated for a late 2022 release from Jackanapes Press.

DAN SAUER is a graphic designer and artist living in Oregon. In 2016, he co-founded (with editor/publisher Obadiah Baird) *The Audient Void: A Journal of Weird Fiction and Dark Fantasy*, which features his design and illustration work. Since 2017, he has worked extensively on book covers and interior art for Hippocampus Press and other publishers. His art often takes the form of surreal collage and photomontage, as pioneered by artists such as Max Ernst, Wilfried Sätty, Harry O. Morris and J. K. Potter.

What if the Sleeping Beauty left to make her own life? What if Bluebeard's wife seized the opportunity for justice? What if the witch truly loved Rapunzel? What if Snow White learned the virtues of right rulership from the dwarves, and Jack learned wisdom from the giants?

DIG DEEPER. TWIST THE TALES AROUND. FAIRY TALES ARE REVOLUTIONARY.

NOT A PRINCESS

BUT (YES) THERE WAS A PEA

& OTHER FAIRY TALES TO FOMENT REVOLUTION

REBECCA BUCHANAN

COMING IN 2022 FROM

JACKANAPES PRESS

www.JackanapesPress.com
www.facebook.com/Jackanapes-Press

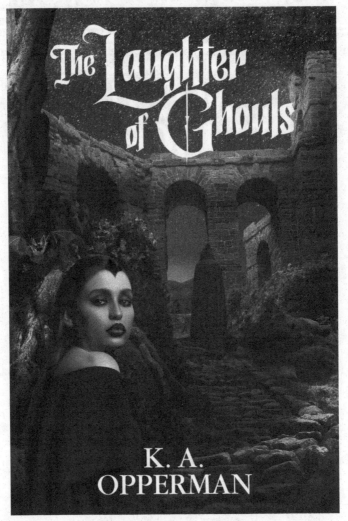